VIOLENCE DAVE
HEARTLESS

Konstantine Paradias

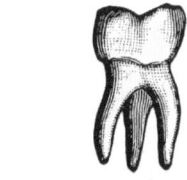

Bizarro Pulp Press
an imprint of JournalStone Publishing

Bizarro Pulp Press books may be ordered through booksellers or by contacting:

Bizarro Pulp Press, a JournalStone imprint
    www.BizarroPulpPress.com

The views expressed in this work are solely those of the author and do not necessarily reflect the views of the publisher, and the publisher hereby disclaims any responsibility for them.

    ISBN: 978-1-945373-95-4

Printed in the United States of America
JournalStone rev. date: June 28, 2017

    Cover Art: Justin T. Coons

    Interior Formatting: Lori Michelle
        www.theauthorsalley.com

ADVANCE PRAISE FOR VIOLENCE DAVE-HEARTLESS

"A balls to the wall mayhem-fest from the first sentence to the last."

—Rodney Turner,
Podcast Host, Microphones of Madness
& *Breath of the Sky* anthology

To Gil, who was about to git gud, but then got a job.

And to that older kid who used to kick my ass at Mortal Kombat whenever I'd visit the videogame store. His prowess taught me the value of cheating.

THE JOB-CLASS LANCER starts to shudder, twenty seconds before deployment. Even through half a meter's worth of hull, I can feel the re-entry burn lapping at my back. Behind us, the world is rising up to meet us, its distant beauty coming apart like a Monet painting.

"It's just 3 kliks from the Heart of Darkness, north by northeast. You get lost, you follow the armor, hear?" Sergeant Ziar says, even as he's loosening up his safety clasps, letting his body hang limply from its harness.

We hang like too-ripe fruit in the diminished gravity, buckles gently *click-clacking* against the spontaneously hardening material of our suits. The lower layer shivers and bubbles with excitement against my skin, tracing my veins with its feelers even through the padding.

"Aaarm!" Ziar calls out and the weapons are out of their holsters and in our hands before we know it: Raptor repeaters and Blitz-guns and rocket-propelled Tearers. The coolant unit from Booker's Czernobog gun starts to purr like a kitten from his back and Guiying's Nine Dragon shooter starts to spin in its chamber, heating the plasma to a boil. From the corner of my eye, I can see them petting their guns, shuddering as they close in for the carnage. They coo softly to their guns, as if they were children.

The lancer unleashes its brakes, going into its corrective spin. This is its death-dive, one final courtesy swoop for its soft payload. Ziar slams the release switch and the floor falls away in pieces, revealing the blur that's the speeding landscape beyond.

"On my mark, we hit the ground running," Ziar says, matter-of-factly, as if he can't feel the wind whipping at his face, can't see the great green rushing strip below, hear the high-pitched whine of the lancer's engines as it slows down from suicidal to mere breakneck speed.

This part always sucks.

"Mark."

The harnesses let us go without a warning and we tumble from the sky like fallen angels. Our armors flood us with oxytocin and the artificial orgasm is almost enough to make me forget about the terror of it all, even as the ground below spins like a belt sander. My muscles relax and my knees buckle but the armor reinforces my back and feet. I barely have time to scream and then . . .

"Impact!" I shout, just as my feet drive into the earth below, my heels digging into the hard ground, tearing through the earth, uprooting the brittle devil-grass. A hundred meters away, Booker is surfing down the hillside, releasing dust devils as he goes. Sergeant Ziar pivots in place, slams his feet against a bit of jutting rock, changes his fall into a run, and waves his arms around like a madman, trying to signal us. Too late, I notice the jagged drop below: a bed of rocks and glass laid out at our feet.

"Booker! Wipeout, down below," I warn him, but he can afford to take the hit; his armor's top-of-the-line assault material, made to shelter his mushy little body even if God were to slam His fist down on it. Not so much with mine.

I search for anything to let me cut down some speed-a jutting bit of rock, a curvy incline on the slope—finally, I see the crooked, blackened shape of a tree sticking out of the ground, its roots still clinging onto the dead, dry soil that bore it. Reaching out, I grasp at the branches and feel the husk hold, only for a second, before it's torn out of the ground and sent spinning in the air. Its trunk lands in front of me and starts to buck and heave across the ground, so I dig my heels into the soil and brake to meet it.

The trunk rolls over me and I hold onto it, letting the armor's casing take the worst of it while the world spins madly around us. Twelve seconds into the spin, I turn my body and make the trunk slam hard against the ground, turning it into a makeshift handbrake. We part the earth below us and I notice that the jagged pit has barely slowed down its ascent.

"For fuck's sake, Private," Sergeant Ziar screams through the comms, "just jump!"

My armor unleashes its short-burst jets as soon as I've jumped off the trunk. I hear the tree crashing into splinters against the rocks and the glass, feel the lower layer skitter across me, savoring the rush. I slam across the ridge and I scamper up its face on my hands and knees. Booker crashes beside me like a bolt of lightning.

"Jesus wept, mate, what the hell was that?"

"Prep time, I guess," I pant and Booker barely has time to process it when Sergeant Ziar slams into the ground next to us, his sleek, chrome-plated rifle purring like a kitten in its holster, its row of blinking lights looking so inviting. Without even having to ask, I can tell that he's never fired it; that the rifle's fresh out of R&D. It's been thrown into the fray as a last-minute wonder weapon that will win us our little suicide mission, a sprinkling of originality added to keep the endless looping tedium at bay.

"Private! That was hands-down the most hare-brained case of deployment acrobatics I have *ever* laid my eyes on," Sergeant Ziar says, and I look away from the cobalt blue eyes behind the visor, his twisted jarhead face that screams obscenities at me through the short-range channel. It's not like I can't take being chewed out; I just hate this next part.

"Are you f—" Sergeant Ziar's rant stops halfway through as the burning green projectile tears the top half of his head clean off. There's a drawn-out gurgle on the line, degenerating into a long, drawn out screech and I can smell the sergeant's burning flesh even through the filter. His tongue is lolling in the air, his jaw hinges down like a broken marionette, and the top of his head has been reduced into a burning, smoking ruin. By the time Booker's started to mouth his usual string of obscenities, I've primed, loaded and brought Bielebog up in a single, flowing motion.

"—Uuuuuuck!" Booker howls, his scream lost under the roaring double-barrel thunder of the assault shotgun. Somewhere in the distance, a blubbering thing with a head like a skinned dog whines, its legs blown out from under it by a concentrated shower of slugs, its guts turned into mincemeat.

"Cover's blown. The lancer didn't work," I say, too

soon. Booker just looks at me, his face twisted in horror and confusion just as the distant roar and rumble of the crashing lancer rises from the mountain range at the edge of the horizon. The ground beneath our feet shakes, as the lancer unleashes its burning payload, reducing what I know is an abandoned encampment and a spent hellgate into fine mist.

"How did you know . . . ?" Booker mutters, but I don't bother. Instead, I shift Ziar's dead body, stripping the shiny rifle and the power pack belt off him, counting the seconds down to immolation. His shiny white armor hisses evilly, a stream of green smoke rising from between its plating. Tongues of flame rise up from it as he cooks. The sergeant's body is reduced to a Hiroshima silhouette in the blink of an eye, already swept away by a gentle gust of wind.

"Move," I bark, and Booker complies, blubbering as he struggles with the weight of the Czernobog, scampering across the faded wasteland trail. We're halfway around the hill, headed east, when he finally musters the words.

"How did you know? How did you know the lancer hadn't worked?"

"Call it a hunch," I mumble, hoping that will keep him occupied, but Booker doesn't bite. I'm leading us down the mouth of a gorge, away from the mission path, toward the hidden trails that have been etched into the heart of everything since this entire mess began.

"We're headed east. You're taking us the wrong way," Booker warns and I can hear him running toward me, aching for a fight, fists clenched. I push him away with the flat of my hand, just as the first volley rains down from the top of the gorge. Booker grunts, staggering against the massive weight of his armor, and sees a perfect bone-spear crescent sprout from where he used to be. From above us, there is the awful hyena yipping of the dog soldiers, signaling their attack. They cackle and bark down at us, rattling their jawbone fetishes. I jump out of the way as one of them, a muscle bound alpha, launches its spear down at where I used to be. The rock behind me explodes into powder from the sheer force of the blow and I shoot Bielebog through cover, divining its position through the cloud of dust. A chorus of yowls rises and is silenced as soon as I unload the second barrel.

"Up and at 'em, Booker, old son," I shout over the cacophony of barking from above, running up a hidden crooked path. The dog soldiers barely have time to notice me, still struggling to take in the torn mess that's become of their leader. Below me, Booker shoots something unintelligible before unleashing a ten-second volley from Czernobog, letting a swarm of two thousand rounds streak across the air. Half a dozen dog soldiers explode into mincemeat and the rest scatter, bone-spears shaking loose from their quivers as they go. In a single, fluid motion, I grab one of their weapons and throw it, running one of them through. It stumbles and falters, staring at the bloodied length sticking out of its chest, pawing at it uselessly. Too late, the other turn around. I unleash two barrels into their center of mass with one hand, unloading a clip into their glistening-skinned faces and eyes with the service pea-shooter. Some of the dumber ones try to rush me, running into my hail of bullets. I waste an entire clip in just two braves before they've swarmed me. I twist out of the way of a bone-spear's tip, then smash a dog face into a shower of teeth with an elbow jab.

One of the dog soldiers tries to play it smart, bobs and weaves around me while I crack its packmates' skulls, then jumps over the ones writhing in the dirt and looks for an opening. Unsheathing its claws, it nicks at my armor, looking for an opening, jabbing at the Kevlar weave under my armpits and neck, searching for a way to dig into the soft human meat under the polymer shell. I let it come close, expose my shoulder, and let it swipe at me with its crooked claw. It tears into the living layer of the armor and through the skin and muscle. The pain is a burning, vicious thing that jabs at my brain and makes me feel alive.

No hurt like the first, I find myself thinking in a dead man's voice before I reach behind me and slam the dog soldier on the ground, crushing its teeth against a rock. It growls and tries to run, but I smash my boot into the base of its neck, shattering its spine. The dog soldier writhes like a worm, too broken to even howl in agony. At the other side of the gorge, the dog soldiers have scattered, their vanguard already cut to ribbons. They're looking to rush ahead of us, across the craggy, lifeless wasteland to warn their masters. Maybe they think they can bring back enough reinforcements, drown us out by sheer numbers.

One of them, a grizzled creature dressed in the pilfered armor of a forward scout, turns to look at me. It bares its teeth and starts to hiss a curse when the entire world is suddenly blanketed in shadow.

We turn to look at the shape that's flying across the face of the sun, Booker and I; at the massive, winged thing that sings like a whale, its silver-scaled skin covered in undulating tentacles that grasp hungrily at the air. It swoops down from the heavens, swiping at the dog soldiers, reaching for the biggest concentration of screaming meat and popping them in its slit mouth like they were candy. I hear the dog soldiers yip and scream for mercy before the gnashing, awful teeth reduce them into a shower of gore.

"Goddamn it, what *is* that?" Booker howls and I wish I could make sense of it. But it's all been abject madness for so long that I just let the horror wash over me, let the awful sight of flying flesh slowly normalize in my mind, until the singing behemoth flying in loops around the sun is just a bit of backdrop.

"It doesn't matter. On your feet," I tell Booker and I move across the narrow ledge, headed his way, but he won't have it, not any of it. He stomps his feet as he heads for me, picks me up by the shoulders and presses his visor against mine before hissing.

"We're going back, you weird little bastard. We're going back to meet with the rest of the team and there's nothing you can do about it."

"Team's as good as gone, Booker. They're probably getting torn apart as we speak. Brass messed up their intel, sent them into the thick of it."

"How can you know?" Booker howls, spit flying against his visor. "How can you fucking know?"

Above, the behemoth stops halfway through its weave across the sky and dives, whistling through the air at us, six eyes locked onto the two tiny, screaming forms below. Its massive skull smashes through the rock, bringing its enormous frame down on us. Tentacles whip at the air and grasp at us clumsily, searching for the screaming, flailing meat. Booker shoots without even thinking, unleashing a full battery into the behemoth's face, tearing through its cheek and popping an eye. It roars, more enraged than in pain, and thrashes into the gorge, whipping at the hillside and bringing a hundred tons of rock down onto the path.

I grasp Booker and we outrun the dust, trip across the stubborn roots of walls and fields of powdered glass and I wonder what this place was called, before the world went tits-up and died, before the skies were ripped open and Hell came to Earth, wiping us out in our billions as it went.

"Where are you from, Booker?" I ask when I can no longer feel him thrashing against my grip.

"What kind of bloody nonsense question is that?" Booker says, as he wrings himself out of my grasp. The question's taken him off-guard. He's more confused than he is angry now.

"What's that accent? Caneater? Kiwi? I can never tell you people apart," I say, looking out into the distance, at the far-off swirl of dust hanging over the faint yellow glare of the hellmouth.

"Pa was a big city man, Ma was from Delungra. We went into the desert when it got too bad in Sydney. Came out just in time to see the world burn," Booker says. We trudge across the shattered pavement for a while, listening to the distant sound of machine roars in the distance, then Booker says, "Who put you up to it?"

"What do you mean?" I ask, as I help him up the next ridge.

"Are you black ops? Some kind of weird psy-ops guy? How did you know the lancer was going to fail? How did you know the brass had messed up?" Booker asks, and he's no longer on edge. Maybe the armor's hit him with a wave of endorphins, just enough to make him mellow. Maybe he's just too spent to give a damn.

"I've just been through this before," I say and hope Booker will leave it at that.

"Piss off. You've never been in the field, you tosser. Guiying ran your file, before they sent us out. You're as green as they come!" Booker says, guffawing.

"Okay," I mutter. That just seems to piss him off more. His hand grasps my shoulder, whips me around. My fist smashes into his chest, the blow reverberating even through the layers of padding. Booker goes down on his knees, panting. I reach out to him, hand stretched to help him up, when he smashes his elbow into my face and sends me spinning. He roars like a berserker as he gets up and rams into me. We roll across the dust and the dirt, smashing a pair of twined lovers as we go, their bones cracking like sticks under our weight. We come to a stop at the base of the hill and I can see the lines of ink across Booker's face light up, too eager for his own good.

"Give me one good reason why I shouldn't beat you into a bloody pulp, you little droog," Booker groans, fist balled and ready to strike, smart-servos whirring as they optimize his blow for maximum damage on impact. Maybe I should let him smash my head in,pound the front of my skull into the mushy grey matter, wrap up this entire bloody mess and save me the trouble of all the awful bloody screaming that's going to come.

"Do it, you bastard," I groan, and I think of the

world beyond burning, think of the soft, yielding surface of crushed bodies piled underneath my feet, my hands shaking as I struggle with a gun that's so hot it's making the skin peel off my palms and I just want it to be over right now, so I hiss, "Do it! Do it now!"

Something bursts out from the ground below us. It stretches its long, segmented body toward the heavens, clicking its mandibles at the sky. When it's uncoiled, it teeters against gravity, whips its spindly legs into the air and finally tumbles down, crashing toward us. Booker unleashes a half-second burst from his jet-pack, *wooshing* out of the way. In the dust cloud around me, I flail blindly, trying to roll out of the way, searching for Ziar's stolen energy rifle. Too late, I fumble with the holster, as the insect-demon lands on my leg and smashes it. The armor shoots me up with a wave of oxytocin before the worst of it can knock me out. Even through the numbness, the agony is overwhelming.

"Too soon, too soon, goddamnit," I moan uselessly and the insect-thing whips toward me, the lower half of its woman-face blossoming into three sets of jaws, green goop dripping from beneath its lolling tongue. The ground beneath bubbles and hisses and I know what's going to happen as soon as it's sunk her fangs into me. One hand still struggling with the energy rifle, I reach for Bielebog and try to level it. The monster snaps at it, almost playfully, grips it in its jaws and send it flying into the distance, then spits a gob of acid just as I release my service gun. Its ceramic surface hisses and pops in my hand as soon as the gob lands on it, so I toss it right back at it. The beast is taken aback by the tiny screaming thing that tries to reach out blindly, grasps its jaw and tries to twist it down on the ground. My fist slams into its too-human cheek, slams into its eye, but I know I've barely even stunned it. In the blink of an eye, it's got me caught in its mandibles and flinging me into the air in a swift, whipping motion and I can almost feel my spine whip around, headed for its wide open maw . . .

And then Booker's Czernobog rips a stream of bullets into its carapace, tearing at the soft meat inside, and the woman-thing yowls in agony. I fall in slow-motion, watching it whip its head around to face Booker, his bullet swarm hanging in mid-air, the insect-thing's gob of acid loose and arcing across the sky to meet him. Without thinking, my hand moves like a blur, releasing the energy rifle as I fall and I know there isn't time to let Booker know what's going to happen next.

The insect-thing buckles as I land on the base of its neck. Wrapping my legs around it, I ride it like a bronco and stick the energy rifle's barrel into the tiny opening in its carapace, against the soft meat below, then pull the trigger. A row of brilliant blue lights flashes across the rifle's stock, unleashing a stream of blue-hot plasma into its innards, tearing through its flesh, unleashing a jet of cobalt dragon-flame out into the air. The insect-thing barely has time to register it's dead, so I grab onto its mandibles with a free hand and tug it back, rip the exit wound open, and let the black blood spray into the air like fine mist to help it along the way.

I drop to the ground and hobble on my broken leg, up to my eyeballs in painkillers and adrenalin, toward Booker's teetering form. He's let go of Czernobog, his left hand clutching at the hissing mess of charred flesh where his right arm used to be.

"God no, God, how did it-" He's moaning and I run up to him, grasp his hand and press my body against the sizzling flesh, against the creeping living layer of the armor that sinks its tiny, needle-like teeth in and weaves itself over his flesh. Booker chokes up, struggling to make sense.

I press my visor against his and say:"Don't look at it. Just don't look at it . . . . "

It's strange, how this part never gets any easier. Booker collapses in my hands and I help him down to the ground, feel him shudder and kick at the air beneath me, listen to his breath come out in long, drawn-out gasps.

"Where'd my hand go? Goddamn it, where the *fuck* did my hand go?" he whimpers, and I reach down at the base of his armor, tapping the tiny valve on his spine, unleashing a wave of euphoria into him, drowning him in bliss. Booker relaxes in my arms while I release his service Dragoon handgun, undo the straps of the Czernobog, and remove the safety latches that will let me take his armor's Azoth core. Booker grabs my hand, halfway through pawing at his armor and hisses, through his blissful grin: "Save them, you shifty little bastard. Save them."

Booker's eyes glaze and he relaxes, his legs kicking at the ground one final time. The ink on his skin burns too late, struggling to animate him, but the armor's killswitch has already been tripped. I rip the core from his body and drag Czernobog off him just as he bursts into green flame. He turns into a corpse-dust outline, already blown in the wind. From somewhere in the distance, a murder of lazily gliding scavengers begins to glide towards the dead insect-thing. I check my busted knee, watch it as it slowly pops back in place, the living layer of my armor sinking feelers into the broken flesh and cartilage, replacing it with its own, sterner stuff. I'll be up and running in a minute, too late to get away from the scavengers, so I decide it's time to try something different for a change.

The insect-thing's flesh is soft, almost pliable, easy to tear through. Outside, the crow-things circle the dead giant, pecking at its carapace, their tiny, vestigial arms pawing at its plating to reach into the glistening carrion underneath. I hear the alpha hiss at the young upstarts, pecking them off the juicy bits in the center, hear it sink its beak into the tender musculature and tear long, thin strips off the beast. The alpha makes a show out of gobbling them up, teasing the youngsters forced to contend with the chewier, rougher meat. A young adult, relegated to omega male status, is forced to lean into the shredded neck-meat of the dead beast and make do with the bitter spoils.

The scavenger's beak slips into the flesh, narrowly grazing my armor, and I grab it, clasping it shut. The omega male struggles to pull out, twisting against my grip, but I pull it deeper into the wound, sliding across the slick offal, moving up its body. It's not a huge specimen, but it looks like it can carry me a good chunk of the way to the hellmouth.

"Easy there, boy . . . " I coo at it, patting the feathered strip of flesh between its eyes. The omega male flinches at that, whips its head back and caws, dragging me out into the open. Its brothers gather around to look at their fumbling jester, struggling against the bucking gnat that's climbed up its skull. They watch as the omega jumps and tumbles against the clanking creature on its neck, throws it on the ground and moves in to skewer it with the tip of its beak, then jump in horror as the tiny parasite blows the top of their brother's head off in a peel of thunder.

The omega male stumbles, tries to look up the blasted mess that's become of the top half of its skull with its one good eye, and finally topples into the dust.

Holstering Bielebog, I grab Czernobog out of its hiding place in the giant's wound and bring it up just as the rest of the murder moves in toward me, beaks clacking eagerly. I pull the trigger, letting a full-bore blast unleash into the carrion eaters, letting fire and lead spray out to tear away at them, smashing their brittle bones and stripping away their flesh. They tumble out of the way, all torn and bloodied, and when the minigun's barrels finally fall silent, its ammo belt spent and its coolant system hissing evilly, the alpha pounces.

Its beak punches through the armor plating effortlessly, tearing through the living layer and into my belly. It rips into my guts as it goes, grazing against my spine. The burning, tearing sensation is so much that the pain doesn't even register. My brain just shuts down and I lean into the blow, let the alpha get carried away by its own momentum, then ball my fists together and swing them into its eye. It pops, exploding into a stream of clear ichor, agony exploding into its primitive brain.

"All you had to do . . . " I say as I twist its beak, make it flap uselessly onto the ground, " . . . was stay the hell out of it."

My fingers dig into its eye and I rip it out of its skull. The crow-demon is swept up in a shower of white-hot agony. It jumps away, its beak unleashing a stream of black blood onto the blasted earth, the flow already stemmed as the armor's living layer starts to knit my torn body together, making it bigger, better, faster, stronger.

"Eat up, boys. Plenty more left before we're through," I groan at the armor, and it chirps happily as it goes to work, leaving me free to struggle with the alpha male, to make a harness out of Czernobog's ammo belt and wrap my legs around its neck in the spare moments of agony. Bucking my hips, I whip its head back and the crow-demon takes to the skies, teetering against the whipping wind. I feel its body move lithely beneath my feet, correcting its course for some old familiar haunt, but I won't let it, tugging at the harness and choking it until it's lined up with the mile-high glowing pillar of light emanating from the hellmouth.

Below us, the world is a still life panorama in burnt orange and grey set against a blood-red sky, the devastation dotted with white where the winds have exposed a killing ground, where the dead have tumbled and fused together into a mess, two years into the apocalypse. From above, they look like a grim mandala, some occult arrangement whose meaning is just waiting to be cracked but I can never look past the bleached arrangement of skulls in the center, can never seem to focus beyond the distant whistling of wind through their eye sockets. The sound of it almost lulls me to sleep. The armor jabs me with a shot of alpha-PVP into the spine, a "victory shot," the kind they've dialed in just for special situations, like *hanging over the earth with a sucking gut wound* kind of special.

I ride the high, letting the armor lock my joints into place around the crow-demon's neck, allowing my muscles to relax and my brain to stew in the gunk. My eyes roll back and for a second, the awful, screaming carnage fades and my life isn't an endless charnel house gallery, my hands don't shake from fighting against the roaring, bucking stock of a gun. This time, I wade knee-deep in the dead and I can't smell the shit and the offal, and the sky above me isn't the blood-red that's seeped in from Hell but a faded blue, the kind that lingers in old photographs, streaked with the white contrails of passing jetliners.

Hell is real, and it's coming this way; the first necronaut's words echo in my head like a mantra, played over and over again in a thousand iterations from boot camp and historical archives. These are the words of a man that crossed from the land of the living into the big hereafter and found that we all end up in the same place: a vast nightmare land where our souls waft across it like clouds, where we are snared by alien predators and we weave across its forests like hummingbirds.

The necronaut crossed into the afterlife armed with the best technology that the most brilliant minds of Earth could provide, strapped into an armored vehicle that carried him across the extreme, unforgiving terrain and let him reach the distant places where Hell's handful of intelligent tribes had managed to carve out a meager existence.

Perhaps the necronaut had thought he could come into contact with the people of Hell; show up on their doorstep like a god-king and impress the masses with simple parlor tricks. Perhaps, he must have thought, he could be the King of Hell, the Lord of the Hereafter.

But the tribes of Hell tricked him, stole his vehicle and chased him into the unforgiving wilderness, the biting trees and the fields of flaying poppies. They hunted him down on their six-legged steeds until he lost them in the desert of powdered glass, subsisted on bitter water and carrion for months and finally made it back to the land of the quick where, it turned out, only an hour had passed.

It took the first necronaut six hours to go over his tale. By then, the scientists realized too late, Hell had already pilfered their technology and was probably considering an invasion. How it must have looked: one of the measured, quiet types silently losing their cool, shooting up from his chair and screaming for someone to close the goddamn door, just as the first helltank burst through with two thousand dog soldiers following in its wake.

The first battle for Earth lasted three hours before the last dog soldier was routed and the helltank was finally stopped. Five thousand people were burnt to ash, along with the surrounding countryside. By the time the gate's power feed was finally shut, another gate opened up in Instabul.

Then in Krakow, turning the sky above Europe red.

Then Kyoto and Bangladesh and Papua, Oymyakon and Cairo, unleashing electrical storms across the world, spewing an army of Hell's soldiers into Earth, their own cruelty enhanced by adapted stolen human technology. Their hordes descended on mankind like a tidal wave, wiping away entire countries as they went.

Within a week, Asia was burning. Within a year, the death toll had climbed up to two billion. For every new piece of experimental tech mankind threw into the fray, Hell would create a countermeasure within the week and the tide of battle would sway once more.

So the few people still alive and in command decided to send another necronaut into Hell to see what knowledge they could glean from their invaders, how they could adapt their own blasphemous technology to save what was left of the species. Sixteen hours later, the necronaut returned, mad and wizened beyond his years, with a head full of forbidden knowledge and said:

We've got the bastards.

Except it took an entire year's worth of work before anyone could adapt the second necronaut's mad rambles into reality. A year of work and a lot of good men and women fed into the meat-grinder, with the survivors culled as their bodies were inked with the strange whorls of Hell and encased in writhing armor, their performance and agony documented until, finally, only twelve remained.

"How many?" I groan, but the crow-demon just caws instead of an answer. It's gliding on the updraft now but I can tell it can't go on for much longer. Maybe I can make it fly until it's collapsed, bringing me half a klik closer to my target, save me a bit of legwork. I run my fingers across the fresh patch of scar tissue on my gut, feel the rough, almost scaly skin there, and I wonder how much more of it's going to replace me before it's all over.

"Just a little bit longer. Then it'll all be worth it . . ." I tell the crow-demon as I pat it on the top of the head. It croons, turning its blinded skull to point at something behind me and I turn, too late, to see the cloud cover above me part and the face of the

Behemoth dip into view from above, covering the sun. Its jaws snap open and shut with barely a flicker, and suddenly the crow-demon's gone from the neck up. The ammo belt whips into the air, no longer holding onto anything as my transport starts to fall like a stone and the world rushes up to meet me.

The crow-demon's corpse goes stiff as it drops, the rushing wind whistling against my helmet. The armor begins to flash nonsense graphs at me as it struggles to calculate the best possible way to keep me from splattering on the ground. The ammo belt flies out of my hand, snapping at the rushing Behemoth, with maw open and ready to snatch me up, already hot on my heels. I've never seen this kind of beast before and seeing that there's something new thrown into the equation—I can't help but laugh.

Beneath us, the blasted landscape starts to sprout more details as it comes into focus, revealing a long line of marching soldiers, clad in their clacking, clanging finest gear. They waver and start to scatter as the Behemoth's shadow falls on top of them and I wonder how many can make out the man riding on the dead carrion eater that's speeding toward them.

Reaching down, I grasp the crow-demon's wings and snap them up, braking in the air. It doesn't slow me down too much, but it lets me veer away from the Behemoth andaim myself at the scattering demons, then ram them with the dead carrion eater. A few notice me as I come in, try to shout a warning, but by then they've already been smashed against the dead crow-demon, piled up along with their brethren. Above me, the Behemoth takes a sharp turn and climbs into the heavens, already wise to my little bait and switch maneuver.

The armor releases a burst from my boot-jets just as the pile of dead and dying demons starts to slow the crow-corpse down, and I launch up into the air ahead of them, with Bielebog and the Dragoon blazing. By the time I've come to a skidding halt in front of them, I've dropped a dozen of the bastards, spraying them with flying hot lead as I go.

Bielebog's shell-chamber rolls with a deep, resonating *kthunk, kthunk* in my hand, shells flying, as a bull-demon brave lunges at me, its curved horn poised to strike. A chunk of its skull explodes into fine mist and the slug's scattershot blows two of its brothers off their feet. I blow the kneecaps off an armored brute with a mouth full of tusks and smash its skull with a single stomp of my feet. A lithe, snake-headed one leaps up from behind the dead one and I duck beneath it, point both Bielebog barrels up, and shoot without even looking, letting its gore spatter over me.

I'm climbing over the dead now, shooting into writhing stragglers, when something *thunks* into my arm, its jagged edge piercing through my palm and knocking the Dragoon out of my hand. I turn around to see a demon dressed in the torn regalia of an officer, a necklace of severed tongues lolling from its neck, a six-legged grunting mount hissing under its feet. The whirring spear gun in its hand *clicks* into place, priming another round. Hanging from its belt, I can see its maggot gun still in its holster and know that this one wants to take me back to its masters.

"Come on then. If you're man enough," I groan, and the officer charges at me, spear gun aimed high, so I dive out of the way, let the shot burrow deep into his own soldiers, feel him wince as he listens to its cry of agony. Ramming my knee against a dead demon's neck, I grasp it by the top of the head and tug, ripping off the flesh in one motion, throwing it against the charging officer just as it levels its next shot. The spear gun flies out of its hand and I shoot Bielebog too low, just as his mount jumps into the air. In the blink of an eye, it's closed the distance and on top of me.

The mount sinks its needle-like teeth into my shoulder, then twists its neck and throws me off balance. Bielebog flies off my hand and the beast's weight slams on top of me, pinning me against the yielding mass of the dead. Its rider leans in and screeches at me, priming its spear gun. I slap it away with a backhand blow, but the officer *tuts*, making a clicking noise with its forked tongue. Its mount bites into me again, threatening to tear through the armor. It doesn't draw blood but the agony is so excruciating that I lash out with my wounded hand, strike the beast with an open-hand blow that sinks the jagged spear edge into its skull and *thunks* in its brain. Its body goes limp, throwing off its rider's aim, giving me just enough time to reach out and grasp its gun arm, crushing it in three places at once. The officer lets out a long, harrowing screech, blinded by agony. It doesn't even notice how I've pressed its own spear gun against its belly until after the first shaft has shot through its body and severed its spine. It keeps kicking and howling in agony, so I shoot it three more times, impaling its lithe form against its mount's on top of the dead. When it's good and still, I tear the maggot revolver from its holster and hold it up against the sun, admiring its gently writhing, half-machine beauty.

VIOLENCE DAYE—HEARTLESS

"You're new. Why are you new?" I ask it, but the maggot revolver only spins its chambers languidly and trills, gently swaying its trigger. Below me, a bull-demon groans, crushed under the weight of its brothers, so I level the gun and pull the trigger without thinking. A gob of burning, concentrated acid lands on it and chews through flesh, bone and brain in the blink of an eye, before plopping among the rest of the dead, sizzling softly.

"What *were* you doing here? All of you?" I ask the dead before I start to climb down into the mess of broken bodies from the crow-thing pile-up. Something glistens among the dead, softly spilling its coolant from a rent in its reinforced casing. I reach for it, ripping the battered box out, tearing off the lid . . .

"Aren't you a beauty?" I ask the bare-metal gun in the box, encased in its shock-absorbing packaging. I don't even have to check its serial number to know its name. Savoring its reassuring weight against my arm, I check its empty plasma feed, all too eager to store another payload. In an instant, my priorities have changed. This is a portable doomsday gun, the kind whose deployment in the field used to be a war crime. It's a wonder-weapon, the first and last of its kind. I feed Booker's stolen core into its chamber without even thinking. So much for plan A. The gun grasps it lovingly, presses it into the chamber, and starts to power its miniature particle accelerator. Its deep thrum turns into a purr and I check the underside for a name, finally find the word embossed in its underbelly, a little mythological joke.

"Typhon," I say and strap it behind me as I make my way up the ridge, across the dead, and down the narrow rocky passageway. The hellmouth's light beckons to me across the killing fields and I look down at the haphazardly strewn maze laid out below me: the angular plasteel and cement ruins held together by twisted girders, infested with some of Hell's clinging, parasitic flora. It looks so much like a dead petri dish, like the demons attempted to grow a city on Earth but it just wouldn't take. Even the ground beneath their feet would reject them.

In the distance, something explodes in a shower of green flame and I can hear the echo of Guiying's Nine Dragon gun reverberating in the air, feel it calling to me. I signal to her through the armor's OS and she responds, her blackened and bloodied face filling my UI.

"This is forward team Sigma requesting immediate assistance, who the hell is this, copy?" she howls over the thunder of her guns. Behind her, I can hear Gennady's guns almost drowning out the distant screams of charging demons, their steady explosive pulse tearing through flesh. Looking past the projection, I can trace the distant dust clouds, almost smell the faint pink mist mixed in it.

"This is Al, team Sigma. Hold tight," I reassure Guiying, whose eyes are only now coming into focus, taking me in. She grits her teeth.

"Where's the rest of your team? Where's Sergeant and Booker?"

"Sergeant was killed shortly after impact and Booker's out. I'm the only one left."

"Figures we'd be stuck with the greenhorn. Any signs from the other forward teams?"

"Not a peep. Could be they're laying low."

"Could be they're dust already. Can you make it to my position?" Guiying says. A holo-display map flashes across my visor as she feeds me the data. I don't have to look too hard to tell that her position's probably swarmed with demons already.

"Aye-aye, ma'am."

"Then move your ass, new fish. Sigma team out."

Her face flickers out of my point of view and I let the armor run a few quick calculations to find the quickest route possible. A 3D directional arrow pops up just above my point of view and I prime Bielebog, bend my knees, and prepare to go into the mother of all kill-runs. Across the armor's living layer, tiny stingers find pressure points in my muscles and jab at them, filling them with their black tar. Across my body, the ink burns and I feel almost invincible as I launch myself down the path, running across a rock outcropping and launching myself into the air. Beneath me, a bobbing swarm of brain-snatchers turn their eye-stalks to look at the howling, bloodied creature that's dropping at them, then unleash their methane jets to get away.

The first one deflates on impact, its rubbery skin collapsing, its organs turned to mush. A double-barreled blow from Bielebog sends two flying as their jets are released, and I jump into another retreating brain-snatcher and sink my arm into the soft patch of meat on top of its skull, grasping blindly in the gunk for anything to hold on to, settling for a ropey length of knotted muscle and tugging roughly at it. That seems to do the trick. Shooting off four more batteries, I watch the brain-snatchers disperse, screeching in horror while my mount starts to bob into the air, slowly descending into the killing fields, toward the writhing mass of demons piling up to crush team Sigma with the press of their own dead.

I jump off my brain-snatcher just as we pass over a mounted demon officer, turn my head to watch as the snatcher mindlessly extends its pincers to grab onto its head and slams its stinger into the base of its skull. The officer howls in agony as the dead meat on its head weighs it down, bringing it crashing into the ground, and I hit the ground running, letting the armor and the living layer pump their own unholy power into my legs so I can thunder across the ground. Without even thinking I slam into one of the brittle glass and plastic walls and burst through on the other side, Bielebog blazing, hand reaching for the maggot revolver. A platoon of demons screech to warn their brothers but it's already too late. Slugs have ripped and torn through their head-meat. Concentrated acid already burns into them.

They only see a blur but feel my boots crush into their skulls as I run across them, smashing teeth and popping eyes as I go. A screaming mass of flesh and bone, hovering on an anti-grav chair, shoots a mini missile barrage at me, and I run around its cronies, let them be annihilated in a shower of flame and shrapnel. By the time it's realized what I'm doing, I'm already behind it, shooting Bielebog point-blank into its power generator. It whips into the air before crashing and exploding into white-blue light.

An armored demon skitters at me, its pincers at the ready. I smash my knee into it, making it buckle down onto its knees, exposing the row of terrified dogsoldiers and yipping lizard-things halfway into priming their weapons. The worm revolver unleashes its burning payload, while my leg stomps down on the back of the armored charger's head, turning the soft brain matter into green and white mush that spills through the cracks.

All around me, demon reserves begin to explode into showers of red and burn, their reeking, bleeding forms rushing past me, turning into a howling kaleidoscope, and the armor jabs me with its reward shot, sending waves of pleasure through me even as I hop and turn around still-twitching arms and kicking legs.

I feel I'm teetering on the edge of a mind-shattering orgasm when something explodes next to me and I'm sent flying through the air, my visor's targeting system flashing nonsense warnings as it tries to make sense of whatever the hell almost hit me. I'm still tumbling through the air when its arms finally grasp me by a flailing leg and pull me up against its huge, heaving form.

"Aren't you a huge bastard?" I ask the beast, my head still swimming as it brings my face level with its own hissing, snarling mug. The entire beast is a towering form made from muscle and taut, leathery skin, its arms and legs covered in crudely grafted armor. Two enhanced waldos bearing rocket-launchers extend from its back. I pull up Bielebog and shoot at it, but the slug explodes against a wall of burning white light. The demon grins at me before its arm slams into my chest, caving my ribcage in a single blow, sending me flying across the dead. I black out in the moment before impact, then wake up to the distant sound of its hydraulic rotors whirring as it stomps toward me.

Searching through the dead, I grasp at my maggot revolver and shoot, sending a jet of acid to hiss across the force field, then a full-bore shotgun blast that hisses uselessly against it. I watch the force field's beehive pattern hiss and sputter for a moment before I unstrap the energy rifle and send a two-second burst into it. The demon stutters as the force field fizzles and the plasma-heat bleeds through.

"Got you now, you bastard," I grin as I unleash a full stream of energy from the rifle, letting its white-hot plasma crash like a wave. It shoots off it, burning the ground beneath it, splashing around my feet, and I feel the armor around me burning, feel it hissing even as its thread-like tendrils weave my bones into shape, fill my collapsing lung, and swim through my bloodstream. The demon roars just as its force field finally gives up the ghost during the energy rifle's final salvo, a wave of concentrated plasma washing over it, setting its meat and machine parts on fire. It howls in agony, too blind to even notice me running across its body, squirming as I slam the energy rifle's butt against its chest plating, smashing chrome and steel, exposing the spinning power core hidden away where its heart used to be. I reach inside, grasping it, and feel its power washing over me, sending the armor into overload, making the living layer howl with power. The demon whimpers, aiming its rocket launcher arm at me, but I whip it away, let the projectile explode into the distance, let it watch and howl in horror as I rip the core out of its chest and let its power run through me, making the armor glow like the midnight sun.

I redirect the power back into the demon and watch it stop mid-howl, its eye-sockets bursting with electrical flame before its skull explodes into a pillar of white-hot fire. The power launches me forward as I go and I hover above the ground, wreathed in flame, launching myself into the air above the killing fields. The armor's gyroscope system keeps me perfectly balanced on top of the barriers as I run across them, watching the crowd of demons rushing to Sigma's position stop to stare at me.

My hand balls up into a fist, index and middle finger forming an imaginary gun barrel, thumb cocked. I aim back at them and go:

"Bang."

A surge of pure energy shoots out of my fingers like lightning, cuts though the demons like butter, and I make another finger gun, shoot down at the blindly retreating monstrosities below, see them get ripped to shreds, their torn limbs carried off on some invisible tide of energy.

The wall in front of me explodes into flame, a battery of flamethrowers unleashing their payload to stop me. Some of Hell's foolhardy champions, armed with their writhing flame lances, charge through the smoke, weapons drawn. The first three are reduced into ash in a single finger gun sweep but the next one manages a blind thrust before its head is swept clean off, its lance-tip running through my shoulder, shattering the bone into fragments. Howling, I tumble with it into the mess of demons, watch as they stampede all over me, their makeshift spears poised to strike. My hands go up defensively and I unleash a burst of power, throwing the bastards off me, letting them splatter on the walls around me. Others explode into flame, five rows deep.

The energy inside me shoots out blindly, missing a charging bull-demon by a wide berth. I spin out of its way and stomp down on the small of its back, shattering its spine before pushing my fingertips against its skull and cooking its brain. The power is waning and running wild and I have a rough idea how I can focus it.

"I won't lie to you, Jim. It's gonna hurt like a bastard," I groan before I grasp the flame lance's haft and tear it off me, watching the energy burn through the wound, keeping the armor's living layer at bay. Howling in agony, I press the flat of one palm against the energy surge and line up the flame lance's tip with the other.

Too late, the charging demons realize what I'm doing. The vanguard is about to signal the retreat when a wave of white flame explodes across their ranks, siphoning the pilfered excess energy into a single wave of destruction. The armor's OS blinks and fizzes out and I feel the pneumatic harness power down, trapping me inside half a ton's worth of metal, leaving me alone with the skittering, hungry, living mass, already hard at work devouring and replacing muscle and bone with something far better. My body begins to ache something fierce and I feel the blood *thumping* inside my skull and I know what it's like to be dying by degrees, to be cooked alive inside a doomed bag of skin and bones and muscle.

"I've had worse," I lie to myself but I can't really be sure. I think of the times I've cragged my legless body across razorwire, skin sloughing off as the napalm digs into me. I think of the long, choking, drowning death as the nerve gas eats away at me and the thousand long deaths I've been through, the countless times I've felt the spinning mouths of bore-rounds as they've tunneled into my flesh. As if excited by the memory, the living layer bites into me like a too-eager lover; the ink burns its way into my musculature and my body tenses up, struggling against the dead weight of the armor.

"Air. I need air," I say, choking up, my hands struggling with the deadlocked latch on the helmet, panting as I struggle to free my face just so I can feel the choked air against my skin. I tear at the latches and let the visor fling open and the still wind is cool against my face, despite the overwhelming stench of demon flesh. My exposed skin is prickling with the leftover power still lingering in the air. I stomp across the last stretch of the killing field and I want to cry as I stare up at the burnt orange sky, but my eyes won't let me. I'm trapped here, inside this meat, and I want to scream, to fight it, but the armor's systems power up and the visor comes down and I'm alone with my own skin again.

"Please, just one more second . . . just . . . " I whimper, but the visor locks in place and the 3D directional arrow blinks to show me on my way, to the distant, fading rumble where Team Sigma are taking out the demon stragglers pushing for the attack, waiting for reinforcements that have long since been cut to ribbons. The last one, a skittering little thing with torn cockroach wings comes running around the corner, its tail-end still on fire. I slam elbow-first into its chest and press the maggot revolver against its pincers, pulling the trigger before it's had a chance to whimper.

"Shhh, it's over now," I tell the hissing, dissolving mess on the ground as I turn the corner, to face the blasted moonscape that Gennady and Guiying are standing. I can see them perched higher up, a neat pile of still-smoking dead arranged beneath them. I watch Gennady make the rounds, looking for any near-dead. When he finds them, he presses the pneumatic jackhammer against their skulls. There's a gentle *whirr* and then a *woosh* before the front of their skulls explodes outward in a shower of bone bits and wet chunks and he moves on to the next one.

"Late to the party huh, new fish?" Guiying shouts from her perch and I just nod, waving to her. Gennady pauses, a screaming demon's skull cupped between his hands, and shrugs.

"Better late than never, Corporal," Gennady says, and the demon's jaw and part of its face explode in a shower of gore.

"Brass messed up the drop point. Sent us almost five kliks off course. The mission's FUBAR and we're going to have to signal a retreat. We need to set up a retrieval beacon so we can get the hell out of here, you get me?" Guiying says while watching me climb up across the dead toward her, weighed down by the Typhon, Bielebog and the worm revolver strapped on me, my armor dented and shattered in places, dried and burnt gore still clinging to it. I'm standing a few feet away from her when she's finally taken me in. "God, where have you been, new fish?"

"Don't wanna talk about it," I say and that seems to do for Guiying. She's always the same, no matter what iteration: the hard-boiled caretaker, stuck behind enemy lines, out to protect her blubbering little school of psychos. I've watched her go the same way a thousand times and I still know that I'm going to miss her like a bastard.

"This," Guiying says, holding up a compact cube in the palm of her armored hand, "is an emergency beacon. Put it in a high place, pull the trigger, and it'll send out an immediate extraction SOS. Brass will have us outta here in a jiffy. Gennady and I are too weighed down by ordnance to make the climb but . . . "

"Just point and I'll jump, Corporal," I say. Guiying seems almost shocked to hear the eagerness in my voice, maybe expecting to go through the motions of following through with a bit of jarhead motivation, but I know we have barely two hours before our position is flooded with more demons fresh out of the hellmouth. She loads the coordinates into the armor and the OS blinks again, pointing at a nearby hill, a column of thick funerary smoke spreading up from its peak.

"You don't have to do it, if . . . " Guiying starts to say but I'm already moving toward the target, carrying a little bit of ordnance that's not even supposed to work, that's supposed to be there to give us hope, make us think we're more than just a bunch of meat grinders with opinions to them. Before too long, I'll be up on that hill, trying out a load of useless frequencies that will get me nothing but static and Guiying and Gennady and I will be headed for the hellmouth, guns blazing.

I'm stomping up the incline when the cube suddenly lets out a soft whistle that interfaces with my armor, lets me know that it's picking up a signal from who knows where. My fingers start to work the holographic interface and the cube whistles softly again, letting me know that somewhere up in the night beyond the sky, someone's listening. I run a quick test on the frequency and it checks out.

There's someone there.

For the first time ever, there's someone there.

My climb turns into a sprint and I pump my legs up the incline, toward the bonfire, my eyes darting to the ticking clock on the bottom-right corner of my visor. The satellite will be above us in three minutes, ready to bounce our communication, and the brass will scramble from their bunker and send a dropship our way, and Guiying and Gennady will be safe before they know it; who knows, maybe I can signal the rest, make them come to me. Maybe no one else will have to die.

Maybe none of us will have to go to Hell this time.

Maybe this will be the end of it.

The blubbering mass of flesh and metal peeks its awful compound head from behind cover and blasts my position with a wave of crackling yellow energy in the blink of an eye. I tumble away from its path, but the blast wave sends me flying, almost has me rolling down the hill into the hundred-meter fall below.

Without even looking, I pull up Bielebog and shoot blindly, aiming for the rough position of the blubbering demon, listen to its howls of agony as the slugs tear chunks off it. Looking up, I see it priming the energy cannon grafted into its gut for another shot, thick power cables glowing with energy as they feed its humming core, and I pull out the worm revolver, shoot a gob of acid into them. The substance tears through the insulation and the blubbering thing howls in agony as white-blue streaks of lighting arc all over the place, its main gun reduced to a useless hunk of metal.

"I don't have to kill you," I shout at it, guns still primed. "Just walk away."

The blubbering thing opens its compound mouth and howls, its call a mix of hyena yelps and human cries. Out from the smoke, its cronies come rushing out, dog soldiers and bull-demons with their guns at the ready, charging downhill. I prime Bielebog and shoot a single barrel into the charging mess, blowing the legs off the vanguard, and watch the next line of chargers stumble into the salvo from my other barrel. The shots are calculated and clinical, corrected by the armor's targeting system. Those that stumble too close get a face full of the worm revolver.

I check the timer, ticking down until alignment: there's 90 seconds left on the clock and I'm already surrounded by a dozen of the dead and the dying. The compound beast above starts to yelp and I break into a run, legs pumping against the ground, launching me further up. I see it trying to roll out of the way, its multi-jointed hands reaching for something, perhaps a gun, anything to keep me at bay.

At 80 seconds on the clock, I've crossed the distance, climbed up cover, and I'm about to tear the compound beastie into pieces, when a jacked-up bull-demon pops out of cover, a burning hammer in hand. I watch in slow motion as it brings the flaming head toward my chest. I try to roll out of the way, but the blow goes wild, whips around and strikes me on the back, the armor hardening to take most of it. The hammer's explosive charge releases and I'm launched into the air, my spine shattered. The bull-demon's head is torn clear off from the back-blast of its suicide attack. I flop in the air before I finally hit the ground, too numb for the pain to even register, my guns dropping all over the place. An entire company of demons looks down at me as I come crashing down, wide-eyed with amazement that this madcap plan somehow worked.

CATASTROPHIC TRAUMA SUSTAINED. RECUPERATIVE SHUTDOWN IMMINENT, the armor lets me know, and I can already feel the living layer scamper to fix the damage, the armor flooding me with painkillers to keep me from going into shock, the ink burning its occult power into me to keep me going. For once, I am thankful for it. Checking the timer, I've got a minute left and about ten seconds' worth of life left in me, at best.

Gripping Typhon in one hand, I prop it up against my belly and feel it hum with power.

"All we wantedwas to walk away," I groan at the demons approaching my position, their faces twisted by horror as they realize what's humming in my hand. A few braves try to rush me, hoping they can save their skins. "We just wanted to go home."

I slam my elbow into the primed cube, let it send its encrypted SOS message blindly out into the heavens. Typhon bucks against my hand, its barrel transforming into a prong-shape, a ball of pure energy suspended in the air, drawn straight from Booker's own core. I grit my teeth as I watch it gather, feel the vibrations rise as the braves realize it's too late for them to scatter, and finally, there's the release.

Just a deep, *whooshing* noise, hanging into empty air.

The eerie quiet before the blast, and then . . .
FWOOM.

A sphere of perfect white light hovers in the air, moving deceptively slow, its touch disintegrating demons as it passes through them and around them. Slowly, languidly, the projectile begins to dip in altitude, down to earth, where it begins to slowly discombobulate, shudder almost with pleasure, and finally . . .

There's a curtain of white-blue light that burns

with the intensity of a thousand suns draped all around me, spreading outward to blanket the horizon. A rumbling, roaring curtain of pure energy that roars monstrously as it explodes, its backblast turning the demons around me into mincemeat, the forward blast spilling down across the hill to topple fortifications and kill whoever's still lingering in their foxholes.

It fades in the space between breaths, and all it leaves behind is a huge swath of devastation, a line of pure, blackened ground that stretches out almost to the ring of jury-rigged fortifications that surrounds the hellmouth. Even there, some of the outcropping pilfered metal has twisted, melted from the sheer intensity of the blast.

"Well goddamn," I groan, as the armor's cocktail finally floods me and I dive into a deep and dreamless slumber. Somewhere in the distance, I can hear the faint sound of my shattered spine, its fragments scraping together, knit by tiny invisible hands.

" . . . Leaving *him* behind!" Guiying's voice comes into focus as my eyes snap wide open and I see the corporal, fists clenched and teeth gritted, her Nine Dragon gun waving wildly in the air. There's someone else there with her: a black suit of armor, his voice like gravel.

"Dropship bay can't handle this kind of trauma. For all we know, he could be a vegetable by the time we land," he says and I can hear the thick Austrian tone in his accent. A name flashes in my mind-*Ekhardt*-and I have to wonder why the hell he is so important. How come I can't remember him right away?

"So it's more humane that we leave him here? To die in this goddamn wasteland?" Guiying turns and can see my eyes wide open behind the visor, trying to make sense of the situation. I wave at her and try a grin but even that is pure agony. "Oh, for Pete's sake, how much of that did you hear?"

"I can stand. Honest," I groan and look at Ekhardt, trying to read his expression behind his tinted visor. Instead, I see his fingers clenching around his Hadur repeater, thumb gently caressing the full auto fire mode switch. Grasping at the debris around me, I try to pull myself up. My hands flail around uselessly, but my legs won't listen; they just hang there, like so much dead weight, and I realize that I'm probably worse off than I thought.

"You'll just weigh us down," Ekhardt tells me matter of factly. Guiying turns to look at the rest of the suits of armor massed around the blasted hilltop; I can see Gennady and Valter and Kaapo, Hyong and Naseem, their suits marked by burns and dents, their visors popped as they look at the scene, not too eager to weigh in on it. After all, they were also dropped right into the grinder, forced to trek for almost five kliks into enemy territory, only to see their teams wiped out almost entirely.

"I'll just weigh you down," I tell Ekhardt and Guiying. They almost seem to jump at that. I grin, too wasted on armor-meds to care. I know that all they have to do is get in the dropship and go home, to get chewed out by the brass, to start again, with a better plan this time. I can afford to die. Hell, I've started to get good at it.

"Shut the hell up, new fish," Guiying says, rolling her eyes before finally turning to the rest. "All right people, the dropship's landing co-ords are just half a klik away. We need to carry new fish a few kilometers and then we're home free. This entire operation has been shot to shit and we won't stick around to see the end of it."

"How can we know we'll make it down there? How can we know there aren't a hundred thousand more of them, just waiting in the valley floor?" Naseem says, his voice cracked.

"We'll stick together, keep a tight formation, blast anything that moves. The dropship's ETA is in half an hour. We can make half an hour, easy," Guiying says.

"And the cripple?" Ekhardt says. Guiying just scoffs.

"He'll be your gunner. You drop him and it's on your head. Hands off cocks and on with socks, people! We're moving!"

Ekhardt grunts as he pulls me up, letting me piggy-back on him. He runs his harness straps across our bodies, wrapping us together, groaning as he feels the added weight of my guns on his back. Even with the extra hydraulic support from the armor, lugging me around must be a bastard.

"Hi-ho, Silver," I chuckle. Ekhardt just grunts something in Austrian and we start to slowly inch down the incline with the platoon, moving ahead, their weapons primed. Ekhardt's gentle rocking motion is starting to lull me to sleep when I hear him whisper, through the close-range comms channel:

"We're not supposed to make it, are we?"

"It's a suicide mission, yeah . . . " I say, nonchalantly.

Ekhardt doesn't buy it.

"Not *us,* just whoever isn't you," he says and I know he's almost embarrassed to admit it.

"That doesn't make any sense, Ekhardt, why would I . . . "

"Because I've been through it. Before," Ekhardt manages, his voice cracking, "it's always the same. New fish makes it to the hellmouth, everything else goes FUBAR."

"Not this time."

"Why is this time different? What's changed this time?"

"I set up the beacon. Someone was listening in. The dropship's coming," I say, but Ekhardt just scoffs.

"It's happened before."

"No, it hasn't. Used to be, they'd leave us here. Use us up like toy soldiers. Now, it's different. Maybe they're going through this too. Same as we do."

"Or maybe that's just part of it. You ever stop to think of that?" Ekhardt says, his voice dripping with rage.

"It's never . . . "

"There's a horde of them, hidden in the hills. They'll come down, at fifteen minutes ETA. I'll push you up into the hatch, watch as they drag you up into the pod and fly away, while a bull-demon guts me," Ekhardt says, predicting his death down to the T.

"Not this time," I say, but my voice is wavering and Ekhardt keeps going.

"And then I'll wake up and I'll be back in the lancer and they'll drop us back in the meat grinder and I won't go through it again, not now, not fucking ever, you hear me, you bastard?"

"I'll make it stop," I plead with him.

"How? How will you ever make it stop?" Ekhardt says, teetering at the edge of tears.

"There's an end to it. All I have to do is reach it. But not before you guys are all out of this shithole."

"Promise?"

"You bet your ass," I lie. Ekhardt doesn't seem to notice.

The valley below is eerily quiet, with nothing but the sound of our trudging boots breaking the silence. It reverberates all around us, across the dusty rock outcroppings, and is bounced back to us tenfold, a titan's jarhead chant:

Thrup-thrup-thrup-ho, hup-thrup-thrup-fo, we go, like a hungry giant's slogan, all chrome and plasteel and gleaming guns. I can feel my spine's shattered pieces slowly clicking into place, knit together stronger than before, and only now do I wonder how deep those tendrils can reach, or how high. The gentle tickling sensation of my left foot's big toe wriggling in my boot helps keep the paranoia at bay, at least.

"It's just over that ridge. Dropship ETA, five minutes," Gennady offers, and we *whoop* as we crest the ridge, look down to see the cracked crater below us, the ground infested with the brittle red weeds of Hell. A platoon of lingering dog soldiers yips and scatters when they see us coming, scrambling across the top of the ridge. A pair of controlled bursts from Kaapo's Durga gun tears them in half and we watch their bodies flop down, wait for them to stop twitching, before we move on.

"There should be more . . . " Ekhardt says, as he lingers on the edge. "There's too few of them, this far into enemy territory."

"Maybe this place isn't worth jack to them. I mean, it's been blasted to shit already," Naseem offers before launching himself down.

"By what? What the hell hit them here? They

never bombed *this* place . . . " Ekhardt says, desperately trying to make *someone* listen, to stop and think for a moment, but I just pat his shoulder and say:

"It's going to be okay," even as I push down the feeling of ghostly dread that's slowly seeping inside me. This place will be impossible to escape, as soon as we're here. If they decide to swarm us, we'll be stuck to each other without any room to maneuver, and they could just pour into our guns, come crashing down into us until they'd crushed the breath out of our bodies . . . "It's just fifteen minutes until the dropship gets here. We can hold for fifteen minutes."

Ekhardt teeters on the edge of the crater and I can hear his breath coming up short on the comms channel, hear him struggle against a dread that's become second nature to him. When he finally takes that first step, he slides down across the dirt smoothly, kicking up as little dust as possible, moving with a carefully rehearsed grace, and I have to wonder how many times he has been through this already.

How many times have they all had to die? God knows I never bothered keeping count.

I watch Naseem take the harness off his back and bolt it to the ground, his gauntleted hands carefully arranging a series of commands on the holopad. With a series of gentle *clicks* and *hisses,* the backpack starts to expand outward, unfolding a string of servos and machine-parts from its insides, arranging itself into a six-barreled turret in the blink of an eye, an ammo belt dropping from its side into the dust. It's a gleaming thing of perfectly engineered beauty that whirrs softly as it pivots, searching for its targets.

"Might as well break out the big ones, right?"

Naseem chuckles. Beneath me, Ekhardt shudders, and right on cue, something howls in the distance, a lone *yip-yip-yip* sound that's joined by otherworldly shrieks that seem to come closer by the second. Skinned dog-heads and bull-demon horns and armored officer goat-heads stare down at us from the crater's rim.

"Fall in!" Guiying shouts, the Nine Dragon gun rumbling in her arms, and we press against one another, back-to-back, weapons primed. In the air above us, there's the faintest hint of a flicker as something moves across the dust, its camouflage distorted.

"Aaaaim!" Guiying shouts hoarsely as the officers whip the cronies into the charge, sending them barreling down the dust, barely a few dozen strong. My trigger finger itches as I prop Bielebog against my forearm, barrels trained on the first few chargers. The flicker becomes more pronounced, begins to slowly congeal, and I see it slowly assume the outline of a gaunt, floating man and I know it seems somehow familiar . . .

"Fire!" Guiying says, and Naseem's turret explodes with the thunder of its guns, reducing the first line of braves into chunks and tear the rest into ribbons, leaving some unlucky few to roll in the dirt, clutching at their ruined and torn limbs, and dragging themselves into their own black blood. With a noise that's barely above a crackle, the flicker fades and I see someone standing in the air above us, a gaunt, skeletal form with leathery skin, its body a heap of flickering wires, a humming power pack strapped to its back. It moves its long, taloned fingers in the empty air, rips away at the fabric of reality. The air above us tears like a fresh wound and then . . .

"Fuck! Incoming!" Kaapo screams.

Something glistens in the air above our heads, the distant wound-glint of Hell's skies, its endless crimson flecked with streaks of silver and white, swarms of human souls torn from the world of the quick and left to infest the afterlife. The sight lasts only for a second before the first dog soldier falls from the lip of the cosmic tear, his body shifting through worlds, exploding into the land of the living in a brief burst of sickly green light.

Then another comes. And another. An entire platoon of the things, with armored horned officers hot on their heels, a fleet of brain-snatchers floating in their trail. Now I finally know where Hell's reinforcements come from, how they can get to us before we know it and pick us off before we've had a chance to scramble our forces.

"Well, I'll be damned," I whisper and the machine gun salvo begins as soon as the fresh batch of demons has hit the ground. The front line have their heads and limbs torn from their bodies before they can manage to scramble for cover, while dog soldiers, three lines deep, fling their spears at us, the rest bobbing and weaving, using the piled dead for cover. Leaning from Ekhardt's back, I shoot Bielebog point blank into an armored demon's chest, again and again. The slugs ping off his armor, sting more than do any damage, but it makes him drop his guard as Naseem's turret shoots a full burst into his head, tearing it off in strips.

A dog soldier platoon jumps up from the dead and Ekhardt blows half of them out of the air with a wide burst. One of the braves makes it through, whipping at the air, and I smash his jaw with Bielebog's butt, leaving him flopping on the ground. Ekhardt crushes his windpipe with a boot-stomp.

"Atta boy!" I roar, whipping out the maggot revolver, letting a few acid gobs fly high, aiming at a pair of officers huddled behind the dead. They scream and I watch one of them step out of cover, desperately wiping away at the acid boring through his skull and cooking his brain. From behind me, I hear the reassuring apocalypse roar of Guiying's Nine Dragon gun, see its green glow reflected on my suit as a symphony of demon screams rises into the air .

The smell of demon offal and cordite and crackling, burning flesh rises so thick that it even seeps through the armor's filters. Beneath me, Ekhardt sucks in air through his teeth and Kaapo gags, but I take in the smell of it all and know that this is the last time I will have to go through it.

"Just this once. Then I'm done," I whisper as the next wave drops from the sky, the green glow strobing as they materialize en masse, their sheer numbers making the ground beneath our feet quake as they come crashing down. Valter and Kaapo drop to their knees, locking their barrels into place to compensate for kickback, and pull the trigger. A fine red mist, flecked with strips of flesh, rises from the attackers. Ekhardt and Hyong and Gennady let loose with a full battery. Around us, the screams become a constant, jumbled cacophony, background noise for Armageddon.

I unleash Bielebog into the mass, letting loose an entire slug cylinder, and watch it fly off the gun. Bringing the shotgun down against my waist, to the armor's portable armor generator, I shoot the worm revolver into the press of bodies.

"Reload!" Guiying screams above the din and I turn, shooting blindly over her, a gob of acid striking a charging bull-demon in the stomach, the agony making him back into his dog soldier entourage. Guiying's Nine Dragon gun is red-hot, its barrel looking almost dented. The thing must have gone way past the limit R&D would ever recommend. Beside her, Naseem is aiming his railgun, shooting a bolt of kinetically-augmented death to pierce through the attackers, then reloading his railgun. Bielebog *dings*, fully loaded, and I bring it up in one fluid motion, aim and shoot while letting the armor worry about where the shots land. From the corner of my eye, I notice the turret's perfect machine coordination and notice that we've stopped our own screaming, started going into the mantra.

Aim. Correct. Bang.
Aim. Correct. Bang.
Aim. Correct. Bang.

Ekhardt stomps over a dead demon officer blocking his view, climbs further up to rain burning lead down on the rest, howling something unintelligible in Austrian, his voice crackling from the repeater's kickback. I laugh at the absurd noise and feel my legs tingle, the sensation returning as my spine locks back into place.

The green light strobes again, a warning flash before a curtain of dog soldiersappear. Burning green streaks of energy shoot out from behind the cover of the dead, flying across the corpse-smoke sky.

"Incoming!" Gennady screams, and we pull away from each other, pulling up the torn dead from around us for makeshift cover. The half-torn brain-snatcher body in my hands *thunks* with a deep, meaty sound as the shots come in, again and again, the flesh and muscle tearing into confetti in my hands from the savagery.

Everyone starts screaming and I turn to look, watching Kaapo howl at the length of spear sticking out of him. He's barely snapped the shaft when a half-dozen blasts tear off his arm, punch through his armor and rip apart the meat below. His body goes limp and I can see his eyes glaze over and Kaapo goes away, just for a second.

Then the ink starts to burn across his skin and he's back again, but not entirely there. From the corner of his eye, Ekhardt notices and lets out a moan as the animated remains of Kaapo start to stomp up the dead, taking blow after blow, letting the spears tear into the meat, letting the blows burn, his gun shooting blindly into the living and the dead alike. His rampage lasts for almost a minute before a random blow cuts him in half and his legs just kick at the empty air. When the armor's self-destruct mechanism triggers, the legs burn fiercely and collapse into a heap of ash.

The armor's living layer gives a little love-tug to my nervous system, as if to give me the go-ahead.

"Cut me loose!" I scream at Ekhardt.

"I thought . . . " he mutters.

"I'm done! Cut me loose!" I howl. Ekhardt's thumb unclasps the harness and I watch the world slow down in the second before I hit the ground, feel unseen pinpricks run all over me, pumping me full of methoxetamine, filling my mouth with the taste of pennies as the roar of carnage around me ebbs away and everything begins to slow down, moving at an almost geological pace.

My feet pound the dirt below and my arms reach

for my guns, priming them with a flick of my thumbs. Releasing a controlled burst from my boot-jets, I turn my sprint and jump into an overarching launch above the corpse-wall and I hover above the massed demons like a goddamn war god.

"Urrah!" I howl and they see me, too late, just before I'm hidden behind Bielebog's baleful two-barrel glow and the worm revolver's final salvo rains down into them. Their bodies slam on the ground and I let gravity take over, allow it to bring me crashing down on an officer and his mount like a steam hammer. Their spines crack under my weight. Their men fly all around me, burning and blasted, as I pull the trigger, spinning like a dervish. The worm revolver clicks, its payload finally spent, so I grab it by the barrel, bring the handle down on a dog soldier that's stumbled in too close, smash it through his eye and leave it buried in his skull.

The dead begin to tumble onto the ground, perfectly choreographed, and I jump off my crushed target before it's collapsed, feel my boots stomp on a bull-demon's skull, cracking his curved horn. I tiptoe across skulls like a jesus lizard, half-running and half-flying over them, aiming, correcting, *bang, bang, bang,* letting the slugs tear away at demon flesh.

I'm halfway across the crater, three dozen dead beneath my feet, when something smashes into my gut, throws me up in the air. In the brief instant of muted agony, I notice the armored horned demon that's struck me across the chest with its bone-club, sent me flying up in the air. Bielebog's out of my reach, but I don't bother with the gun. My hands grasp the demon's horns and I tug his head forward, into my knee, feel his face get pulverized against the armor's polymers, the sucking sensation of blood streaming down my leg. The demon tumbles back and I grab Bielebog in its descent, give him a full-bore blow into his exposed neck, nearly tearing his head off.

When I fall back down, my drop cushioned by the dead, I feel my insides churn. Bile rushes up from under me and spills out from my throat. Something must have torn up in me, but I trust the armor to handle the worst of it. From above, a brain-snatcher moves in and I side-step out of its path, let it strafe past me and blow its top off. Bielebog clicks again, out of ammo.

"Reload!" I howl, the bile spilling out of me, and the sickly green glow flashes again, stronger than ever. A new batch of demons comes in, their skin and muscle a mess of fused metal, crackling with power, their reinforced gauntlets clawing at me. They swarm at me and one of them, a gaunt thing with jackhammer hands, clambers on top, brings its arms against my helmet and gets a good one in. The blow is almost apocalyptic, throwing my head back, jangling my brain, the lower half of my visor exploding into pieces.

All around me, they jam their misshapen fingers into the plating, try to tear away at the armor, their blows rattling the casing. It holds, but the flesh is weak. It bruises and cracks in places and the muted agony comes into the foreground and I can't reach Bielebog, can't reach my gun, and the jackhammer-hand demon climbs onto my chest, lines up its arm with my exposed face . . .

And gets blown off its feet by a screaming bolt of metal.

"Clear!" Naseem's voice rises above the din as he aims, shoots, charges again, clearing the demons off me. The drugs wear off and I'm high on pure adrenalin, kicking the dead and the dying off me, ripping Bielebog from the dead. Naseem gives me a thumbs-up and then his head is surrounded by a miniature hell-portal halo and a gaunt half-metal beast reaches out from the other side to rip his head clean off. The ink of his body glows and the flesh continues to stomp aimlessly around, even as the blood geysers up into the air. They sizzle and burn as the armor's self-destruct flame envelops them, reducing him to ash.

"You twisted little fuck!" I howl at the demon hanging in the air, and I shoot at it but the slugs ping off an off-blue shell of energy. It lets out a shrill, high-pitched noise that sounds almost like a cackle. With a flick of its wrist and a flourish, I watch it slice into the empty air, tearing the barrier between worlds wide open. From across Hell, an insect-demon bursts through, its howling woman-head clanking with reinforced metal jaws. It sprays acid as it goes, letting it rain down on the dead and the dying, and I roll to dodge the worst of it, feel a few drops pitter-patter on the armor and burrow through the reinforced polymers.

"Come on, sweetheart! Let's dance!" I roar at it and shoot a round from Bielebog, letting the slugs glance off its carapace to get its attention. It whips its head at me, twisting in the air as it skitters down, mandibles rattling at one hundred times a second, and I weave across the demon stragglers, let the beast barrel down across them, flinging their bodies, watch it stumble as it trips over a pile of bull-demons, their limbs blown apart, and I jump across its mandibles, thump my boots across its face and hold on to the long, ropey hairs dangling from its skull. From somewhere behind the pile, I can hear Guiying roar as she unleashes another burst of green flame that laps up at the insect-demon, making it jump in fear.

Tugging at its hair, I make the insect-demon rear back into the air, its legs wriggling uselessly. It bucks underneath me, spraying acid, a jet spattering over the gaunt demon's shield. With a swift kick to the back of the head, I make it stumble down onto the corpse pile, drive it across the massed dead, lap around the crater. Somewhere in the distance, there's the off-pitch whine of a dropship's engines as it begins to break in its atmospheric descent. The gaunt demon notices it too, its taloned hand beginning to weave another portal.

"Up you go, sweetheart," I grunt at the insect-demon and slam my elbow into the back of its head, make it jump across the crater, tug its hair to force its head back, letting it spit acid at the gaunt demon's shield. It crackles with blinding brilliance as we close in, the mandibles *click-clacking* at it, cracking across the force field. Panicking, the gaunt demon whips its hand around and releases a quick portal toward the insect-demon, teleporting half its head into Hell, leaving its body to shudder and begin to drop uselessly toward the ground . . .

. . . clearing my run.

The gaunt demon hisses as he sees me sprinting across the carapace, boots stomping over the shells, Bielebog primed in hand. Its shield's glow is still overwhelming but it's begun to waver and the gaunt demon starts to weave another gate to whip at me, but by the time it's flung it I'm in the air and on top of him, fists slammed against the crackling wall of light. Pure, unfiltered power crackles through me like I've grasped a live wire, makes my heart skip a beat and my skin crackle as I dig my fingers inside and rip apart the shell made from light, tearing it wide open.

The gaunt demon screams and I shove Bielebog into its mouth, savoring the sight of teeth flying as the barrels knock them loose.

"Good game," I say and pull the trigger, watching as the slugs explode the back of its skull outward, sending grey matter and bone fanning out in every direction. One of the gaunt demon's eyes explodes out of its socket, a gust of flame sizzling as it pops out of its skin. Its body begins to shudder, arcane machinery unloading its payload, spitting a shower of sparks that turns into a jet of liquid flame. The half-woven portal bursts into being, unchained, and the green glow unleashes a torrent of tumbling demons into the crater, scurrying to our position in droves, so I ram my hand into the exit wound on the back of the gaunt demon's skull, into the pulverized meat, and aim its still-twitching corpse like a gun, making the portal's rim twist and turn, feeling it fight me.

Ebbing and squirming like something out of a child's nightmare, it rolls across the dead, swallowing them whole, twisting and dicing the stragglers in the rim between worlds before it finally collapses on itself, leaving a few dozen dead and a handful of survivors scared shitless. The gaunt demon's body finally goes limp and we drop down among the offal, our bodies charged up with arcane energy, just as the dropship finally whips across the air above us, coming in for its final round.

"Evasive maneuvers! We're getting the hell out!" Guiying howls across all channels, and we begin to climb across the dead, heading up so we can maybe get snatched up by the dropship, get flung across the planet, back home and away from here.

"Arm hooks!" Guiying shouts and I watch them release their hooks, hold them up as they begin to crackle, instantly magnetized. Ekhardt looks at me knowingly.

"Hook's shot, Corporal. Can't make it," I say and Guiying's about to scream her head off at me when the lone bull-demon bursts from the dead and grabs Ekhardt by the ankles, thrusts its head up to drive the curved horn into his gut. One shot from Bielebog tears off his head.

"New fish, you stupid little . . . " Guiying starts to say, when the dropship whips by and they are all swept away, dangling under it. It begins to reel them into its padded interior during its slow-down phase, before it slingshots back into orbit, and I watch it hang there like a distant jewel when Ekhardt's comms channel flashes at me:

"'This won't change anything," Ekhardt says, already choking.

"Might as well give it a shot," I tell him as I watch the dropship dip in the air, correct itself, its engines priming with a few test thrusts to correct its course. Its whine rises in pitch, about to tear through the clouds, when the awful shadow falls across the face of the sun and the Behemoth's yawning maw pops up from behind the jagged mountain range, its teeth clamping down on the dropship. From the comms channel, I hear the reinforced hull and everyone's bones crackle and pop like popcorn. Ekhardt and the rest don't even have time to scream before its teeth finally click shut.

There's a certain flavor to rage.

Not the tinny, biting taste of murderlust, or the tangy, lingering chaser of fear.

It's a cold, awful thing that clamps down on your heart until its beat becomes a slow, geological crawl; it makes your balls shrivel and go halfway up your stomach, slowly inches a live wire across your spine and pumps enough juice to sanitize you.

To make you into a machine.

The Behemoth twists and turns into the air, lets out a sound like a whale-song. Drums start to beat in my head and I run toward it, away from the piled dead, through the rocky jumbled terrain and into the open dusty field. I don't sprint; my movements are the steady one-two-three tempo run, a gentle slow down followed by quick bursts of speed that carves away at the distance. I've caught up with the Behemoth's giant shadow before I know it, skirting across it. One look up and I notice its bloated underbelly, the glistening wound-lips of its slitted mouth, the clacking teeth that rain down gore and dropship coolant.

Releasing the mag hook, I power it up and shoot Bielebog up at the Behemoth's patches of exposed skin. Even the full double bore battery won't hurt it badly, but it will sting hard enough for it to notice me.

Pausing in its murder song, the Behemoth pauses halfway through its aerial dance, floats away and pivots in the air. Four sets of eyes focus on the tiny creature below. I shoot again, letting the muzzle flash betray my position. The Behemoth dives toward me, bellowing, and I speed up my run toward it, letting out a long howl to drown out its own thrumming moan. The dust around it whips up into a cloud and I drop down, slide across the rocky ground just as it tears through cover, and stick the mag hook up.

I'm snatched up toward its slitted mouth just as the Behemoth whips upward, slipping through its closing teeth, into the wet and dark mess of its mouth. The mag hook drags me up against the roof, where the dropship's shredded underbelly has gotten stuck between the Behemoth's teeth, and I kill the power feed, letting my momentum carry me up into its gullet, the fleshy ridged canals of its throat.

"Release terrain hooks," I tell the armor and two dozen metal talons jump out from the soles of my boots, rip into its throat-meat, steadying my ascent. The Behemoth's mouth lolls and it wriggles its tongue, trying to pick at the persistent bit of food that's stuck in its throat. One cough could flay me alive, so I press Bielebog's barrels against the flesh and pull the trigger, squint as I feel the Behemoth's blood and chunks spatter against my exposed skin. They taste sour and biting, like month-old meat. When I've punched a hole through its throat, I stick both fists into the wound and rip away at it, tearing apart flesh and parting muscle. The armor hits me with a wave of alpha-PVP and suddenly the awful, hot press of the Behemoth's innards isn't there anymore. I pull myself up into the throbbing, *thunking* guts of the Behemoth, and I crawl, scramble, run across its guts, and the press isn't so bad. The beast chokes and hacks and coughs as it feels me running under its skin, blasting holes into its guts, and even though I am wading ankle-deep in its blood, hurting it like a tiny death-god, the entire mad thing feels almost casual.

"I'm a zombie worm, you bastard. Snaking up to your brain," I say and break into a cackle while I'm ripping through a curtain of tissue, up a wall of fat, following the long trail of the spine up to the skull. The alpha is making my step so springy and careless that I misjudge the leap across the ribcage, drop through it and slide across the pumping meat of its lungs. The Behemoth exhales and the lungs' motion throws me across the air, crashes me against muscle.

"Stupid. Fucking stupid," I groan, struggling to get up on my feet, feeling my ears pop as the lungs prepare to blow again, and all around me there's the shuffle and skitter of feet, the click and hiss of needle-like teeth. In the large, echoing halls of the ribcage, sound becomes a nonsense jumble that comes from every direction at once, so I suck air through my teeth and shoot blindly out into the darkness. Something is blasted back, its chest torn open. In the brief muzzle blast, I can see mouths with rows of teeth arranged like lawnmower rotors, long and sinewy bodies, covered with loose vestigial limbs, pressed into each other in a compound arrangement.

Like an idiot, I shoot into the press of them again and try to count their numbers, to see beyond the press of their vanguard beyond. Two poor bastards get torn to bits, their death cries calling out to the rest of the brood, who pounce for the attack, and I'm about to shoot again when . . .

THUMP

The lungs expand, sending a burst of air through the Behemoth's torn throat. We launch into the air like ragdolls and I watch the wriggling parasites' bodies whip around me, their teeth clamping down on my armor's hard layer. I smash Bielebog's butt against one's head and watch it pop like a zit, its teeth coming loose. Twisting to slam into the muscle wall, I crush two more and blast the last one as it whips from my legs, hanging on by its tail.

I'm landing, drenched in gore, and below me the parasites have raised their rotor-mouths, ready to catch me and tear me apart, one tiny bit at a time, so I reach out against the muscle wall, plant my feet, and use the boot-jet to launch in the air against the lung. Its soft, yielding meat cushions the impact and I try to grab onto anything, but the surface is too slick and the parasites simply skitter closer, clambering on top of each other to reach me.

"No, no no, no, godammit no," I yell, uselessly, and shoot Bielebog, but it's too little, too late, and behind me there's the Behemoth's awful sucking noise, like a newborn tornado, and . . .

THUMP

The lung-blast hits me like a steam-hammer, sends me crashing down against the ribcage, knocking the wind out of me in the process. Something inside me comes loose and the armor flashes some sort of warning, but I let the living layer do its job, even if I feel a loose, hard piece of bone seesaw in my lungs with every breath. Across the darkness, the parasites skitter and test the air, looking for the persistent bit of morsel in the distance.

Already, a few braves are testing the ribcage, looking to cross to me. I reach to my back and look for Typhon, but it isn't there. A quick area scan by the armor verifies that my last-minute Armageddon option was thrown off its holster during the last cough wave. I'm groaning in rage and agony when a parasite brave's teeth clamp down on my thigh, and I bash my fists into its back and sides, then stomp it until it pops across the ribcage floor.

THUMP

goes the cough-blast and I'm thrown against the back of the ribcage again, smashed against the Behemoth's bones. The armor's living layer groans against me and I know that the pressure is getting too much for it, that another five minutes of this and I'm dead meat, so I have to be out of here before it's had a chance to go.

"Or I can just stop it," I groan and run across the ribcage, ears pricked up to catch the sound of the lungs shuddering, revving up for another fit over the parasite's collective hiss. I barrel into their mass, slamming into their soft bodies, stomping down on them as I go, tearing away from their withered, grasping hands, but their press gets to be too much, the drag slows me down and almost makes me grind into a halt. When their teeth start to form tiny pinpricks across the armor's hard layer, I roar and unleash the boot's jets, blasting some of them away, taking enough drag off me to pick up speed again, to push through them and reach the lung.

But the parasites rush in again and they're on my back, their whipping tails wrapped around my legs, and I'm stumbling, kneeling, and the lungs start to contract again as they prepare to blow . . .

"Please God, let this fucking work," I moan as I unload Bielebog into the lung-flesh, let the slugs punch through the softer tissue. Something rips in the dark. There's an awful sucking sound and then a long, crunching noise as the torn lung sucks the air around it, taking the parasites in, tearing them off me, and sending them to career through the air and splatter against the wound, the entire swarm of them blasted into a wall of wriggling flesh as the lung crumples like an old paper bag. Typhon is there, laid out under the wall of the crushed dead and dying.

I climb across the howling, wriggling wall, across the collapsed lung in the chest of the Behemoth, sprinting up its shoulder blades while the beast turns in the air, puzzling at its own agony. Beneath me, its heart pumps harder than ever as the agony overwhelms it. Maybe I could blast it now, blow a truck-sized hole into its chest, kill the Behemoth in a single, apocalyptic display of power. But the sensation of the loose bit of bone slowly knitting itself back in place tickles the back of my brain and I know that that's not enough; nowhere near good enough.

"But that's too good for you, you bastard. Isn't that right?" I say to no one in particular. Somewhere in the world beyond, the Behemoth lets out a cry of agony, perhaps as it feels me stomping along the length of its spine, making my way across the tight weave of muscle, and finally I reach the back of its skull.

And ram myself against the bone, roaring as loudly as I can, smashing my body against it, slamming my boots against it, watching it crack and cave. When my shoulder pops, two minutes into the blow, I slam Bielebog into the opening, wedge the barrels against it, and blast a hail of slugs into the crack, letting the muzzle-flashes seep into my eyes and blind me as I watch it come apart, as I feel the Behemoth waver in the air in agony, and I know there isn't much time left before it tries a suicide run—maybe a dive into a mountain side or down into the ground, some way to lessen its agony—but I won't let it.

"Not yet. Not just yet," I roar as I look down at the gently glistening meat behind the skull. I pry the layers of bone apart and watch the grey matter pulse in front of my eyes, so I reach out, sink my hands into it, tear it off in chunks . . .

. . . They're in my mouth before I can stop myself, big chunks of grey matter that stick to the roof of my mouth and fill my throat with the taste of demon-blood. I rip them off in droves and chew them up, let them fill me, and I imagine the Behemoth feeling me as I burrow through its skull, making it blind and deaf and dumb, and finally it begins to sink like a stone, careening toward the ground.

When we crash, we do it in a shower of tearing flesh, cracking bone. Beneath us, the dead are pulverized and the dying howl in agony. The sudden lurch sends me crashing through the brain and I stomp out of the muck, against the yielding curve of an eyeball, so I kick at it once, twice, three times, until it's popped out of its socket, and I rise out of it, a newborn war-god, death-god, bathed in the sickly yellow glow of the hellmouth that yawns open in front of me, with a thousand demons staring up at me, and I roar, gun at the ready.

"Too late to run," I tell them, bringing Typhon up at them, cranking it up to its highest setting. It whines like a dying beast, crackling with energy. When I pull the trigger, there's barely any back blast. Just the eerie quiet before the storm, the awful lurch as its terrible payload is released into a slow-moving ball of light, and then . . .

FWOOM

The world becomes a mile-high wall of annihilating light that rolls almost languidly, scooping up demons, scattering them into ash as it goes. I watch them get devoured as it rolls across them: the screaming officers and the massed dog soldiers, the scampering half-machine things and the rest of the beasts that uselessly turn for cover.

It takes a long while for the light to die down. When it's finally spent, Typhon's main reactor unit sizzles and the gun lets out its final machine-dirge before it's shut down completely. I don't have to look too hard to know that its main processing unit has melted into a puddle of silicon all over its inner workings in the long second after its coolant system finally gave up the ghost.

Out from the field of ash and dust and charred bodies, demon stragglers begin to rise from their foxholes, guns at the ready. I pull Typhon's trigger and then finally throw it down at them, chuckling as I watch them dive out of its path.

COMBAT SCENARIO 17B: FORWARD TEAM EXTERMINATED. COMMENCING IMMEDIATE RETRIEVAL PROCEDURES, the armor's visor flashes, and a chill runs through me as I feel it rev up its core, reaching out across the air, across layers of meat, into the crushed metal below.

"Don't do this. Goddamn it, don't . . . " I beg, but the armor keeps going, its plating lighting up as the rest of the forward team's armors respond to the signal. Somewhere inside the Behemoth, an invisible weave of power spins through the dead meat, dislodging cores and equipment. Below me, the surviving demons begin to slowly climb up the smashed-up remains of the Behemoth, scrambling to reach the lone gore-drenched human, outnumbered and outgunned. I shoot Bielebog into the first pair of scrambling bull-demons and dive behind the Behemoth's popped, dangling eye just as a horned officer, the lower half of his body replaced by an armored tank body, launches a length of barbed metal toward me. The eyeball pops as it's skewered and the fluids run across my back, sizzling as they run across the pathways of power.

From across the Behemoth's back, the flesh bulges and tears. Ekhardt's Hadur repeater, glistening with coagulating gore from its journey through the giant, flies into my hand and I pop out of cover, unleashing a controlled burst of fire at the officer. The bullets ping across his armor and finally blast his exposed skull into bits.

Stepping out of the hellmouth, a platoon of Hell's freshest soldiers comes stomping out, hot from the nightmare cathedrals—gaunt, eyeless things with pincers for arms, spitting fire; limbless creatures with the heads of birds, hovering on top of platforms, bristling with guns. Eight-legged rolling soldiers with lion-heads, their vestigial arms crackling with power. I've cut down the first row before they've wised up to me. A torrent of crackling green energy flies up toward me, blowing off the top of the Behemoth's skull as I dive out of the way. Out from its blasted body comes Guiying's Nine Dragon gun, filling my hand just as Ekhardt's repeater finally runs out.

"Burn, you fuckers!" I roar at them as I pull the Nine Dragon gun's trigger, watch the flame shoot out in a long, unbroken stream that clings onto flesh as it erupts into a wall of greek fire. They scatter around the kill zone so I turn during my run, switch the fire mode to a projectile launcher, and pull the trigger. There's a deep *thunk*ing noise as the gun unleashes a missile that lobs up into the air and lands among the runners. It mushrooms out into a cloud of green flame that has them screaming to high heaven. One long burst of fire tears through the stragglers at the edge of the Behemoth, waiting to ambush me with their weapons at the ready.

When I've finally released the gun's final blast into a platoon's worth of bull-demons holed up in a nearby foxhole, the air around me reeks of brimstone. The newcomers stare at me, the bloodied madman, dead men's guns flying toward me, Gennady's jackhammer gauntlet locking itself in place in my hand, Valter and Hyong's repeaters clicking into place. I shoot one of Bielebog's barrels into them but they're ready for me by now. The slugs ping off their force fields uselessly. Their retaliation comes in a wave of energy blasts that send me careening through the air like a ragdoll.

OUTER LAYER DAMAGED. COMMENCE EVASIVE MANEUVERS, the armor suggests, but I'm not having it. Stumbling off my feet, I spit blood and roar:

"More power, you bastard," I roar at it. Again, the armor flashes its warning at me, pinpointing the severely damaged places where the living layer threatens to be unleashed.

ARMOR INTEGRITY COMPROMISED. COMMENCE- it says again, but I just reach for the dead man's switch under the visor, rip it clean off. The warning fades away as I crush it under the heel of my boot.

"More power," I roar, and the armor searches through the dead, rips the cores out of their armors, sends them careening toward me through the dead flesh like miniature meteors. I'm reaching out to them when the air around me ripples and I'm staring into a hissing lion head. Its claws swipe at me, tearing through my armor to rip through my muscle, exposing bone.

I scream in agony and drop to my knees, the core flying away from my hand, careening into the distance. The demon's paw slams down on my back, grinding against my spine, and the pain makes me black out, envelops me in deep, impenetrable darkness, and I know that I've been an idiot, that I deserve to die, but the ink kicks in, sending its occult power into my muscles, and my arm shoots up, sending the jackhammer gauntlet's blast right up between the demon's legs.

It makes a tiny yelping noise before the top of its head flies off, its brain reduced into a shower of offal that flies up into the air and turns into mist. Its brothers are too busy scrambling for the attack when the core finally clicks into my armor and I feel the layer suck every bit of juice from it. Somehow, I know it's Ekhardt's.

"More," I tell the armor, even as I feel the surge infuse the living layer, the outer casing crackling with the scavenged energy. A pair of hovering demons move in, spraying burning plasma as they come in. I launch myself up into the air, riding on the wave of power, then twist like a ninja and land on top of one. It caws in horror just before the jackhammer gauntlet slams into its reactor pack. I let my armor take as much of it as I can steal before its battle-brother turns and blasts it out of the sky in an effort to send me with it. I zip through the air too fast for its eyes to see, ram into the flying demon, make it tumble into the dirt, and slam my thumbs into its eyes. It howls in agony as they pop, gurgles uselessly as I rip off its neck and unleash a torrent of power which I drink deep.

The rocket-propelled grenade which breaks me away from my feast barely registers. A half-dozen rockets explode against my back and I spin in the air, turning just in time to see an armored platoon of demons, their bodies bristling with guns. Their force fields take my retaliatory blows, making the bullets *ping* off them uselessly, so I reach for another core, another burst of power. This one is Valter's, and it makes the living layer writhe with pleasure.

"Hurt me," I say through gritted teeth and throw up my hands. The excess power forms a crude shield that causes the demon's rockets to shatter uselessly against it. By the time the smoke has settled, I'm already on them, my armor crackling with power. My jackhammer gauntlet crashes through a force field. One of the demons looks in horror as I fire Bielebog into his brother's skull, then turn and blast his own arm off. The third one is smarter; he shoots me point blank, trusting that his force field will hold as I jump at him. The explosion knocks us both onto our asses.

When I've finally focused, I noticed the demon reaching for something by the hellmouth: a button, sticking out from the jumble of wires snaking out across worlds. A full burst from one of the repeaters turns his fingers into a red ruin. Without missing a beat, the demon shoots its missile salvo at me blindly, blows the ground up from under me. I shoot blindly into the mess and hear the demon scream as it's giving up the ghost.

"Well played, you sneaky little fucker," I groan as I listen to the hellmouth's whine grow in pitch, its infernal machinery revving up. Something stumbles out from the barrier between universes, a towering, gurgling thing that howls like a pile of babies on fire, a nuclear fire burning in its belly.

"I am going to eat you, you bastard," I roar up at the thing as another core flies into me. This one is Hyong's and it makes the living layer bulge obscenely, makes a surge of power shoot into my muscles, permeating me.

LIVING LAYER ENGORGED. CONDITION CRITICAL, the armor warms me pointlessly, and I can feel the layer's alien musculature flow and fuse with mine, feel its power fill me up, and I fall into the armor, become one with it as I stomp down at the beast. With a swipe of its hand, it unleashes an invisible swath of power, a weaponized tear between universes that rips into reality around me. I jump over it with brand new muscles, eliminating the distance, crash into its force field and correct my course, looking for an opening. The beast pivots, releasing a barrage of miniature gates that blow holes into the ground behind me that go on forever. Aiming up with Bieloebog, I point up my fingers like a gun and channel the energy into a cascade of power that blinds it temporarily but doesn't make a dent.

"More!" I howl, and Guiying's core is added into me last and I feel a wave of horror fill me as I realize I've gone too far, given the armor too much. The living layer grows, bulging obscenely, envelops the outer layer, skewers through me and grows under my skin.

Everything inside me begins to boil. I howl as I watch my body become wreathed in crackling blue flame, and I know I must release it or burn forever. I bend my knees and leap . . .

. . . only to fly instead, propelled on a pillar of

flame that launches me upward, pushes me away from the ground even as it pushes upward through me, and I can taste the burning on my tongue so I aim Bielebog again, pull the trigger, and imagine that I am unleashing a double-barreled blast that could scour the Moon, a blast that could sterilize Hiroshima twenty times over.

The shot punches through the force field and tears through the beast, punching a hole through the meat, into the whirring machinery. Somehow, it still teeters on its hydraulic legs, blasts me with a yawning vortex of world that crackles as it crashes against my wall of power. Again, I shoot at it, tearing off its limbs, blasting the legs out from under it. Again, it howls and whips a scythe of energy that tears up the red of the sky, exposing the night beyond.

"Stay. The fuck. Down," I roar at it, and Bielebog charges the final salvo, a beam of concentrated energy that comes down like the fist of God Almighty, crushes the beasts beneath it, then flies up into the heavens, withering in the blink of an eye, leaving nothing but the crackling hellmouth beyond.

The power inside me is already ebbing and I can feel the living layer nibbling into me, the armor still crackling with enough energy to destroy the machinery that's keeping the hellmouth open.

"I can make it go away. Right now," I say to no one in particular, and I can do it, I can finish the nightmare, start anew. I can choose not to step into Hell, to let it all end in this place, knee deep in the dead.

But Hell is just a hand's breadth away from me and its forests are a nightmare landscape of jagged metal, its deserts of powdered glass infested with nightmare cathedrals, its skies swarming with the souls of countless dead, and I know that Guiying and Ekhardt and Naseem and Kaapo and the others are among them.

"One last time. One last run," I tell the armor, but the layer just skitters and the armor doesn't listen and the power ebbs slowly, its roar fading into a crackle. I check my guns but they are all spent, save for Bielebog. I search the dead and tear a gun that the armor knows how to fire from a dead demon and I strap it on my back. Not much of an arsenal, but it'll have to do.

"Then it's over. I'm done, you hear?" I say as I step into the hellmouth just as the gateway begins to waver and collapse, into the great red land beyond the place of the quick. I linger in the space between universes, but there is no answer.

Just the living layers' faint chitter, so much like a chuckle, aching for more.

About the Author

Konstantine Paradias is a writer by choice. At the moment, he's published over 100 stories in English, Japanese, Romanian, German, Dutch and Portuguese and has worked in a freelancing capacity for videogames, screenplays and anthologies. People tell him he's got a writing problem but he can, like, quit whenever he wants, man. His work has been nominated for a Pushcart Prize.

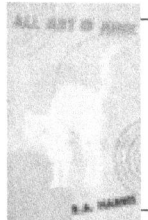

All Art is Junk by R. A. Harris

Lana Rivers, a girl with paintbrush hair, is missing and it's up to Lancelot, her cyborg knight, and his bionic conjoined twin, Cilia, to find her before her evil father, a disrespected artist turned mad-scientist, performs a terrible experiment on her.

Cherub by David C. Hayes

Cherub wasn't like the other boys—too slow, too rough—but he didn't deserve what that hospital did to him, and now he will make them pay.

Skinners by Adam Millard

Los Angeles, the City of Angels. At least, that's what the brochure says. What it fails to mention is the earthquakes. Oh, and the flesh-eating creatures lying dormant beneath the concrete, waiting for the chance to surface once again. Their wait is over . . .

The After-Life Story of Pork Knuckles Malone by MP Johnson

What's a farm boy to do when his pet pig becomes an evil, decaying hunk of ham with slime-spewing psychic powers?

A Lightbulb's Lament by Grant Wamack

A gentleman with a lightbulb for head wakes up in a world full of darkness, hooks up with a beautiful ex-prostitute, and an old man who can heal people; he travels down south to find the mysterious Creator.

PseudoPsalms by Peter Adam Saloman

Bram Stoker nominated author Peter Adam Salomon has laid bare the intricate horrors of the human condition in this poetic compilation; PseudoPsalms: Saints v. Sinners.

Gravity Comics Massacre by Vincenzo Bilof

An absolutely shitty novella involving comic books, aliens, a serial killer, teenagers in an abandoned town, horror-trope dream sequences, and an ending you're going to hate.

Glue by Scott Lange

Sticky bowels and sticky situations.

Ascent by Matthew Bialer

Is the 8 foot tall creature haunting a small town in Iowa in the fall of the year 1903 the product of a hoax and collective imagination or was it one of the first documented paranormal event in America? This epic poem grapples with these questions.

Fecal Terror by David Bernstein

A killer turd is on the loose!

The Fairy Princess of Trains by Christopher Boyle

Danny's mediocre life turns upside-down when his couch starts whispering to him. Then he's charged with a supernatural mission: Rescue the Fairy Princess of Trains.

Terence, Mephisto & Viscera Eyes by Chris Kelso

9 new science fiction stories from Chris Kelso

Bizarro Bizarro: An Anthology

The finest bizarro short stories from 2013.

Notes from the Guts of a Hippo
by Grant Wamack

A rugged journalist travels to Brazil in search of a missing hippo researcher and the notes left behind lead to something earth shatteringly revelatory.

Day of the Milkman by S. T. Cartledge

In a world dominated by the milk industry, only one milkman survives after a terrible storm sinks all the ships and throws the Great White Sea out of balance.

Moosejaw Frontier by Chris Kelso

An unapologetic disaster of metafiction

Notes from the Guts of a Hippo
by Grant Wamack

A rugged journalist travels to Brazil in search of a missing hippo researcher and the notes left behind lead to something earth shatteringly revelatory.

Industrial Carpet Drag by Bruce Taylor

Chemicals make you do great things!

Necrosaurus Rex by Nicolas Day

Necrosaurus Rex tells the tale of Martin, a simple janitor, who takes an unfortunate trip through time, becomes a violent mutant, and the father of us all. There's 14 billion years crushed inside these pages, and most of them are pretty nasty.

The Boy Who Loved Death by Hal Duncan

From blackest humour to bleakest horror, with twisted relish, Hal Duncan's eighteen tales dig into death—and the life that goes with it.

X's for Eyes by Laird Barron

Between the machinations of the disciples of black gods and good old corporate skullduggery, it's winding up to be of a hell of a summer vacation for the Tooms Brothers.

Omega Grey by Seb Doubinsky

When professor Todd Bailer embarked on a psychedelics quest to discover if the land of the Dead really existed, he had no idea he would threaten the cosmic balance of the universe by triggering a real-estate conquest of the new Frontier.

Berzerkoids by MP Johnson

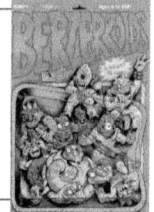

The first short story collection from Wonderland Book Award-winning author MP Johnson

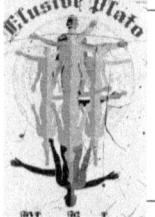

Elusive Plato by Rhys Hughes

The last in a long decadent line of piratical Spanish eccentrics, Bartleby Cadiz grows up in isolation to be as mad, bad and metaphysical as his ancestors. But he feels there is something different about him. What can it be?

Boiled Americans
by Michael Allen Rose

Boiled Americans is a puzzle box in book form, inspired by the violence of living in urban America and exploding the tendency to forget or ignore.

Great American Slasher
by David C. Hayes

Baseball, apple pie . . . and murder.

The Bohemian Guide to Monogamy
by Andrew Armacost

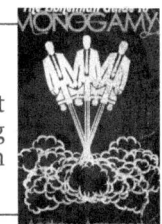

Here, a strange labyrinth of interlinked short fiction assembles itself into a darkly moving novella that deftly explores the bottomless pain and pleasure of love and commitment.

Surreal Worlds edited by Sean Leonard

An anthology of surrealistic compositions created by some of the finest names in genre fiction. A showcase of international talent undaunted by the conventions of language and common narrative structures. Here is timelessness. Here is Surreal Worlds

How to Succesfully Kidnap Strangers
by Max Booth III

Do not respond to bad reviews. If you must respond to bad reviews, please do not kidnap the reviewer.

ADHD Vampire by Matthew Vaughn

He came, he conquered, he was distracted a lot

Static/Orgone by Jamie Grefe

A double-novella of literary grindhouse nightmares and theoretical post-apocalyptic vengeance.

Retch by David Bernstein

What would you do if you were cursed to puke right before you reached orgasm? You'd do anything, right? (You know you would.) Find out what one wealthy, good-looking, playboy will do to try to end his abhorrent curse.

Battering the Stem by Bob Freville

A darkly comic urban crime novella. What would it take to make you beg?

Wonder Weavers by Matthew Bialer

An epic poem about a mysterious sighting in 1896.

Cartoons in the Suicide Forest by Leza Cantoral

When we're dead
You know she'll adore us